Westfield Memorial Library
Westfield, New Jersey

O9-BUA-109

Westfield Memorial Library
Westfield, New Jersey

BEOWULF
MONSTER SLAYER

**A
BRITISH
LEGEND**

ICELAND

ATLANTIC

OCEAN

GRAPHIC
UNIVERSE™

STORY BY
PAUL D. STORRIE

PENCILS AND INKS BY
RON RANDALL

NORTH

SEA

IRELAND

BRITAIN

NETHERLANDS

N

FRANCE

Westfield Memorial Library
Westfield, New Jersey

BEOWULF

MONSTER SLAYER

A BRITISH LEGEND

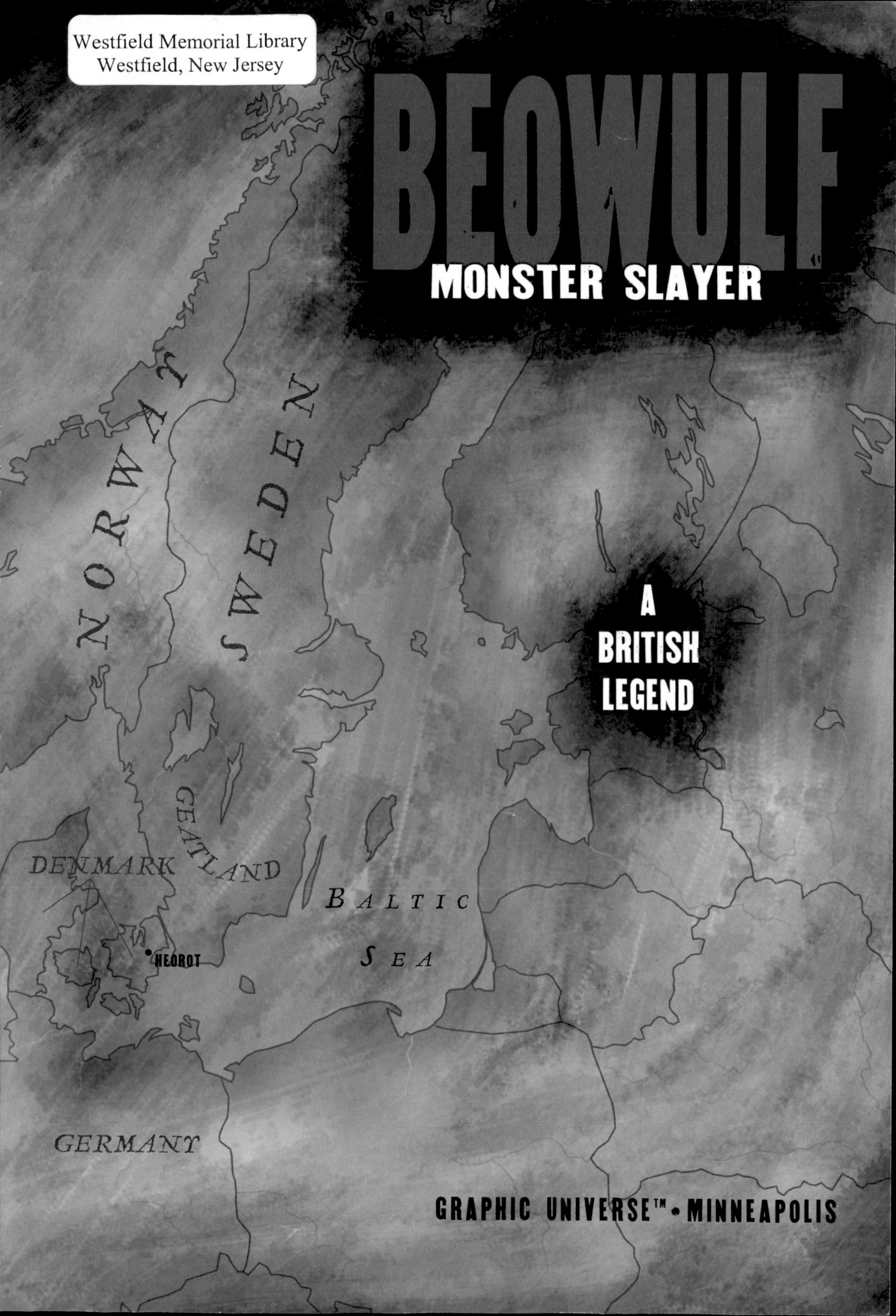

NORWAY

SWEDEN

GEATLAND

DENMARK

•HEOROT

B A L T I C
S E A

GERMANY

GRAPHIC UNIVERSE™ • MINNEAPOLIS

BEOWULF IS AN EPIC, A LONG POEM THAT TELLS OF HEROIC DEEDS. THE HERO BEOWULF'S STORY HAS ITS ORIGINS IN TRADITIONAL TALES FROM THE ANCIENT GERMANIC WORLD. IN THE FIRST MILLENNIUM A.D., GERMANIC TRIBES SPREAD THROUGHOUT THE LANDS SURROUNDING THE NORTH SEA. THIS REGION INCLUDED DENMARK, SWEDEN, AND THE BRITISH ISLES. THUS, THE AUTHOR OF BEOWULF WOULD HAVE HEARD THESE ANCIENT GERMANIC STORIES AT HOME IN BRITAIN.

SCHOLARS DO NOT KNOW EXACTLY WHEN THIS UNNAMED AUTHOR FIRST COMPOSED BEOWULF. BUT MANY THINK IT WAS FIRST WRITTEN DOWN IN ANGLO-SAXON, OR OLD ENGLISH, BETWEEN A.D. 700 AND 800. ABOUT A.D. 1000, ANGLO-SAXON SCRIBES (PEOPLE WHO COPIED MANUSCRIPTS BY HAND) PRODUCED A COPY OF THE POEM THAT STILL EXISTS. THE COPY'S FRAGILE, ONE-THOUSAND-YEAR-OLD PAGES ARE PRESERVED IN THE BRITISH LIBRARY IN LONDON, ENGLAND.

IN MODERN TIMES, BEOWULF HAS BECOME AN IMPORTANT WINDOW INTO THE ANGLO-SAXON WORLD. MANY SCHOLARS HAVE STUDIED THE POEM, INCLUDING J.R.R. TOLKIEN. TOLKIEN WAS SO INFLUENCED BY BEOWULF THAT HE USED PARTS OF IT IN HIS SERIES OF NOVELS THAT INCLUDES THE LORD OF THE RINGS.

AUTHOR PAUL D. STORRIE, ARTIST RON RANDALL, AND CONSULTANT ANDREW SCHEIL USED TRADITIONAL SOURCES TO ENSURE ACCURACY.

STORY BY PAUL D. STORRIE

PENCILS AND INKS BY RON RANDALL

COLORING BY HI-FI COLOUR DESIGN

LETTERING BY BILL HAUSER

CONSULTANT: ANDREW SCHEIL, PH.D., UNIVERSITY OF MINNESOTA

Copyright © 2008 by Lerner Publishing Group, Inc.

Graphic Universe ™ is a trademark of Lerner Publishing Group, Inc.

All rights reserved. International copyright secured. No part of this book may be reproduced, stored in a retrieval system, or transmitted in any form or by any means—electronic, mechanical, photocopying, recording, or otherwise—without the prior written permission of Lerner Publishing Group, Inc., except for the inclusion of brief quotations in an acknowledged review.

Graphic Universe™
A division of Lerner Publishing Group, Inc.
241 First Avenue North
Minneapolis, MN 55401 U.S.A.

Website address: www.lernerbooks.com

Library of Congress Cataloging-in-Publication Data

Storrie, Paul D.
    Beowulf : monster slayer / story by Paul D. Storrie ;
  pencils and inks by Ron Randall.
      p.   cm. — (Graphic myths and legends)
  Includes index.
      ISBN-13: 978-0-8225-6757-8 (lib. bdg. : alk. paper) 1.
Graphic novels. I. Beowulf—Adaptations. I. Randall,
Ron. II. Beowulf. III. Title.
    PN6727.S746B46 2008
    741.5'973—dc22   2006039094

Manufactured in the United States of America
1 2 3 4 5 6 - JR - 13 12 11 10 09 08

TABLE OF CONTENTS

THE COMING OF
BEOWULF

LONG AGO, IN A PART OF SWEDEN THEN KNOWN AS GEATLAND, THERE LIVED A GREAT WARRIOR CALLED BEOWULF. LEGEND TELLS THAT HE HAD THE STRENGTH OF THIRTY MEN AND A BRAVE AND NOBLE HEART.

WHEN BEOWULF HEARD OF TERRIBLE TROUBLES IN DENMARK, HE DECIDED TO HELP. HROTHGAR, KING OF THE DANES, WAS A FRIEND OF HIS FATHER'S. WITH HIS COMPANIONS, BEOWULF SET SAIL ACROSS THE COLD NORTH SEA.

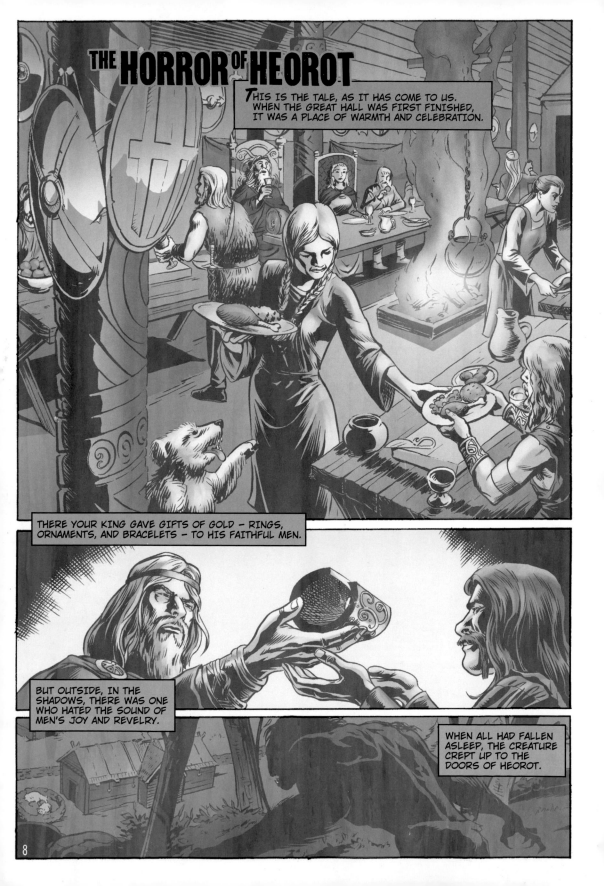

THE HORROR OF HEOROT

*T*HIS IS THE TALE, AS IT HAS COME TO US. WHEN THE GREAT HALL WAS FIRST FINISHED, IT WAS A PLACE OF WARMTH AND CELEBRATION.

THERE YOUR KING GAVE GIFTS OF GOLD – RINGS, ORNAMENTS, AND BRACELETS – TO HIS FAITHFUL MEN.

BUT OUTSIDE, IN THE SHADOWS, THERE WAS ONE WHO HATED THE SOUND OF MEN'S JOY AND REVELRY.

WHEN ALL HAD FALLEN ASLEEP, THE CREATURE CREPT UP TO THE DOORS OF HEOROT.

THE DOOR WAS NO BARRIER FOR THE CREATURE, WHOSE NAME, WE HAVE HEARD, IS GRENDEL.

THOOM

AS THE DROWSING WARRIORS JUMPED TO THEIR FEET, THE MONSTER SNATCHED ONE UP.

AND SWALLOWED HIM DOWN.

BEFORE THE OTHERS COULD DO ANYTHING, HE GRABBED UP A SCORE OF THEM...

FLED...

AND WAS GONE.

FOR TWELVE LONG WINTERS, EVERY TIME SOMEONE DARES TO STAY THE NIGHT IN HEOROT, THE CREATURE RETURNS.

SO, WE HAVE COME FROM ACROSS THE SEA TO LEND OUR AID, TO END THIS GRENDEL'S MENACE.

BY YOUR WORDS AND YOUR MANNER, I CAN SEE YOU ARE HONORABLE MEN.

I WILL GUIDE YOU TO HEOROT, GREAT HROTHGAR'S HALL.

NOW I MUST LEAVE YOU AND RETURN TO MY POST, TO GUARD THE SHORES.

MAY GOD GIVE HIS BLESSINGS TO THE TASK YOU HAVE TAKEN UPON YOURSELVES.

I AM WULFGAR, HERALD OF HROTHGAR, AND YOU MUST ANSWER TO ME.

WHO ARE YOU, THAT COMES TO THE HALL OF HROTHGAR SO BOLDLY? WHY ARE YOU HERE?

I AM BEOWULF, SON OF ECGTHEOW. I AND THOSE WITH ME HOLD HYGELAC OF GEATLAND AS OUR KING.

AS FOR OUR PURPOSE, I WOULD TELL THAT TO KING HROTHGAR MYSELF.

LIKE THE WATCHMAN, THE HERALD COULD SEE THAT THE GEATS WERE WORTHY OF TRUST.

WAIT HERE. I WILL ANNOUNCE YOU TO THE KING.

BEOWULF, YOU SAY? SON OF ECGTHEOW? I KNEW HIM WHEN HE WAS A BOY!

I HAVE HEARD HE HAS GROWN INTO A MIGHTY WARRIOR.

BID THEM ENTER SO I CAN LEARN WHY HE HAS COME!

11

HAIL, HROTHGAR, GREAT AND GENEROUS KING!

WELCOME, BEOWULF, SON OF MY FRIEND! TALES OF YOUR VALOR HAVE ARRIVED BEFORE YOU.

TELL ME, WHY HAVE YOU COME?

TO DO BATTLE WITH GRENDEL! TO RID YOUR GREAT HALL OF THE SHADOW LOOMING OVER IT.

I HAVE HEARD THAT THE BEAST USES NO WEAPONS, SO I WILL FACE GRENDEL WITH MY OWN BARE HANDS.

BUT SHOULD I FAIL AND FALL, I ASK THAT YOU SEND BACK MY ARMOR TO HYGELAC, MY KING.

LONG AGO, WHEN MY BROTHER WAS KING, YOUR FATHER CAME HERE SEEKING REFUGE. HE HAD TO LEAVE YOUR HOMELAND BECAUSE OF A FEUD.

BUT WHEN MY BROTHER DIED AND I TOOK THE THRONE, I WAS ABLE TO SET THINGS RIGHT, SO HE COULD RETURN HOME.

THAT WAS BEFORE I BUILT THIS HALL. BEFORE GRENDEL CAME AND KILLED SO MANY.

NOW YOU HAVE COME, A GREAT WARRIOR READY TO SLAY THE CREATURE MENACING MY HALL.

WE SHALL HOLD A FEAST IN HONOR OF YOUR COMING AND TOAST YOUR BRAVERY!

ONE OF HROTHGAR'S THANES, CALLED UNFERTH, WAS JEALOUS OF THE HONORS HEAPED ON BEOWULF.

SO, YOU'RE THE GREAT HERO, COME TO SAVE US?

I WONDER, ARE YOU THE SAME BEOWULF THAT LOST A SWIMMING MATCH TO BRECCA?

IF YOU CAN'T WIN A SIMPLE RACE, HOW IS IT YOU EXPECT TO DEFEAT GRENDEL?

MY HUSBAND, I WISH YOU JOY AND THAT OUR BRAVE GUEST CAN RID OUR HALL OF THE TERROR WE HAVE SUFFERED.

AND YOU, BEOWULF! I THANK THE ALMIGHTY FOR SENDING YOU HERE IN ANSWER TO MY PRAYERS.

AFTER BEOWULF HAD DRUNK DEEPLY FROM THE MEAD CUP, QUEEN WEALHTHEOW CARRIED IT TO THE OTHERS IN THE HALL.

BEFORE WE GO TO THE SAFETY OF OUR SLEEPING CHAMBERS, I PRAY GOD WILL PROTECT OUR GUESTS AND BLESS THEIR EFFORTS.

BECAUSE THE MONSTER, GRENDEL, WOULD HAVE NO ARMOR, BEOWULF SWORE HE WOULD WEAR NONE HIMSELF.

GRENDEL

OUT IN THE DARKNESS, GRENDEL WAS PROWLING. THE SOUNDS OF CELEBRATION HAD REACHED HIS EARS OUT IN THE DARK FENS THAT HE CALLED HOME.

HATE FILLED HIS HEART AS HE CREPT TO THE HALL, AND HUNGER RUMBLED IN HIS GUT.

INSIDE, THE GEATS SLEPT AND DREAMED UNEASY DREAMS.

ALL BUT THEIR LEADER.

GRENDEL DID NOT FEAR THE BLADES OF BEOWULF'S MEN. HE WAS ENCHANTED SO THAT NO WEAPON COULD PIERCE HIS HIDE.

BUT BEOWULF'S FIERCE DETERMINATION AND STRENGTH SOON FILLED GRENDEL WITH FEAR.

THE TIMBERS OF THE HALL SHOOK WITH THE FURY OF THEIR FIGHT.

WITH ALL HIS MIGHT, GRENDEL FOUGHT TO FREE HIMSELF FROM THE HERO'S HOLD.

WITH ONE LAST DESPERATE WRENCH, GRENDEL PULLED AWAY.

BUT BEOWULF KEPT HIS GRIP.

GRENDEL KNEW HE COULD NOT LIVE MUCH LONGER.

STILL, HE STUMBLED FROM THE HALL, HOPING TO REACH HOME.

WHEN DAYLIGHT CAME, NEWS OF BEOWULF'S VICTORY BROUGHT MEN FROM NEAR AND FAR TO SEE THE TRUTH FOR THEMSELVES. THEY FOLLOWED GRENDEL'S TRACKS FROM THE HALL, WONDERING WHERE HE HAD RUN TO.

BEFORE LONG, THEY TRACED HIM TO THE END OF HIS TRAIL.

SURELY IT IS GRENDEL'S FOUL BLOOD THAT MAKES THE WATERS BUBBLE AND STEAM.

IT MUST BE. AND LOSING SO MUCH, THE MONSTER MUST HAVE DIED BY NOW.

THEY TOOK BACK THE NEWS, CHEERING FOR BEOWULF AND SINGING SONGS OF HIS COURAGE.

STILL, BEOWULF WAS NOT QUITE CONTENT.

I HAD HOPED TO HAVE THE WHOLE CREATURE TO SHOW, SO YOU COULD BE SURE IT WAS SLAIN.

BUT THE WOUNDED MONSTER HAD FLED TO HIS LAIR.

THERE IS PROOF ENOUGH THAT GRENDEL HAS DIED. NO LIVING THING COULD SURVIVE SUCH A WOUND.

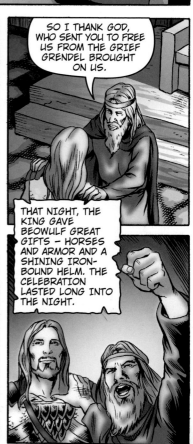

SO I THANK GOD, WHO SENT YOU TO FREE US FROM THE GRIEF GRENDEL BROUGHT ON US.

THAT NIGHT, THE KING GAVE BEOWULF GREAT GIFTS — HORSES AND ARMOR AND A SHINING IRON-BOUND HELM. THE CELEBRATION LASTED LONG INTO THE NIGHT.

COME, I WILL SHOW YOU TO A CHAMBER WHERE YOU MAY REST MORE EASILY. WITH GRENDEL GONE, THERE IS NO NEED FOR YOU HERE.

A MOTHER'S REVENGE

*T*HAT NIGHT, THE DOORWAY STOOD EMPTY. EVERYONE THOUGHT THE DANGER WAS GONE.

BUT WHEN ALL WERE ASLEEP, A SHADOW CAME CREEPING. GRENDEL'S MOTHER CAME SEEKING REVENGE FOR HER SON.

SHE KNEW THAT HER STRENGTH AND BATTLE SKILL WERE NOT AS GREAT AS GRENDEL'S.

SO SHE ONLY SNATCHED UP ONE WARRIOR AND WENT ON HER WAY.

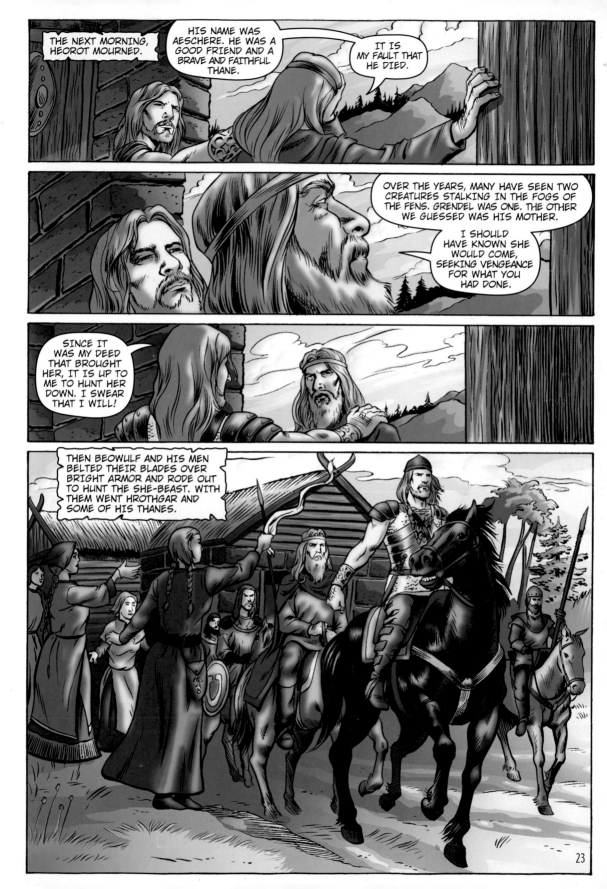

INTO THE LAKE GRENDEL'S MOTHER HAS GONE. INTO THE LAKE I MUST FOLLOW.

SHOULDN'T YOU SHED YOUR ARMOR? IT WILL MAKE SWIMMING HARDER.

IN A LAKE LIKE THIS, THERE ARE SURELY ALL MANNER OF FOUL SERPENTS. MY MAIL MAY KEEP ME SAFE FROM THEIR FANGS.

THEN UNFERTH, ASHAMED OF HIS INSULT TO BEOWULF, CAME FORWARD.

WAIT! LET ME OFFER YOU THIS.

ITS NAME IS HRUNTING.

IT IS AN OLD AND FAMOUS BLADE. NONE WHO HAVE BORNE IT HAVE EVER FAILED IN BATTLE.

I WILL DO MY BEST TO BRING IT GLORY.

GOOD KING HROTHGAR, GENEROUS GIVER OF GIFTS, I ASK THAT IF I DO NOT RETURN, YOU SEND WHAT YOU'VE GIVEN ME TO HYGELAC, MY KING.

TAKE CARE TOO OF THESE FRIENDS WHO HAVE FOLLOWED ME TO YOUR LAND.

24

THEN BEOWULF DOVE DEEP INTO DARK WATERS.

BEOWULF WAS RIGHT ABOUT THE SHARP-TOOTHED SERPENTS, BUT HIS ARMOR TURNED BACK THEIR TEETH.

FINALLY, FAR BELOW, HE FOUND THE HOLE WHERE GRENDEL'S MOTHER MUST HAVE GONE.

HIS LUNGS BURNED FOR BREATH, BUT HE SWAM ON.

FINALLY, HE FOUND AIR.

AND HE FOUND MORE THAN THAT — GRENDEL'S MOTHER!

WHEN SHE SAW BEOWULF, STRONG ENOUGH TO SWIM DOWN TO HER HOME, SHE KNEW HE WAS THE ONE WHO HAD KILLED HER SON.

RRRRRAAAAAAHHHHR!!

EVEN HRUNTING, THAT SHARPEST OF SWORDS, COULD NOT HARM HER.

THROWING THE SWORD ASIDE, BEOWULF STRUGGLED TO FEND OFF HER CLAWS AND TEARING TEETH.

26

THE HERO WAS STRONGER.

WHUD!

BUT THE OLD SHE-BEAST WAS BOTH QUICK AND CRAFTY.

OoooPH!

THOUGH SHE WAS SAFE FROM SHARP BLADES, SHE KNEW HE WAS NOT.

BUT AGAIN HIS ARMOR SAVED HIM.

SNAP!!

27

HNUNH!!

THEN THE GLINT OF A GOLDEN HILT CAUGHT HIS EYE.

IT BELONGED TO A MIGHTY SWORD, FORGED BY GIANTS. WHO KNOWS HOW IT HAD COME THERE?

IN A MOMENT, BEOWULF SNATCHED IT FROM THE WALL!

GRENDEL'S MOTHER KNEW THAT HER ENCHANTMENT WOULD NOT STOP THE GIANT'S SWORD.

BEOWULF KILLED HER.

BUT HER BLOOD ATE AT THE BLADE.

THEN BEOWULF SAW GRENDEL'S BODY IN THE CORNER.

NOW I WILL HAVE REAL PROOF THAT GRENDEL IS DEAD.

BEOWULF HEWED OFF HIS HEAD.

GRENDEL'S BLOOD WAS EVEN FOULER THAN HIS MOTHER'S. IT BURNED THE BLADE AWAY.

THRUSTING HRUNTING BACK IN HIS BELT, BEOWULF TOOK HIS PRIZES IN HAND TO TAKE BACK TO THE KING.

BEOWULF RETURNS!

AND I BRING TREASURES!

ONE MORE GRUESOME THAN THE OTHER.

HAIL BEOWULF!

BURDENED WITH THE MONSTER'S SKULL, THEY HEADED HOME TO HEOROT.

WITH BOTH MONSTERS DEAD, THE SHADOW OF FEAR FINALLY LIFTED FOREVER FROM THE HALL.

TO YOU, KING OF THE DANES, I GIVE THIS ANCIENT TREASURE AS PROOF OF MY PLEDGE.

BOTH MONSTERS LIE DEAD, NEVER TO HAUNT THIS HALL AGAIN.

WE GIVE OUR THANKS, BEOWULF, GREATEST OF HEROES.

YOU HAVE DONE WHAT WE COULD NOT, FREEING US FROM FEAR.

MAY YOU LIVE ALL YOUR LIFE WITH THE SAME COURAGE AND GOOD FAITH YOU HAVE SHOWN HERE.

WITH THAT, BEOWULF TURNED HIS THOUGHTS TOWARD HOME.

TO YOU, UNFERTH, I GIVE THANKS FOR LETTING ME BORROW THE GREAT BLADE HRUNTING.

THOUGH IT COULD NOT WOUND GRENDEL'S FOUL MOTHER, IT IS STILL A WONDEROUS WAR-FRIEND.

AND TO YOU, HROTHGAR, I PROMISE YOU THAT IF YOU EVER NEED MY HELP, YOU HAVE ONLY TO SEND WORD.

YOU HAVE ALREADY DONE MORE THAN I CAN EVER REPAY. I ONLY HOPE THAT YOUR OWN PEOPLE REALIZE YOUR WORTH.

IF YOU OUTLIVE HYGELAC AND HIS HEIR, THE GEATS COULD CHOOSE NO BETTER KING THAN YOU.

BEOWULF THE KING

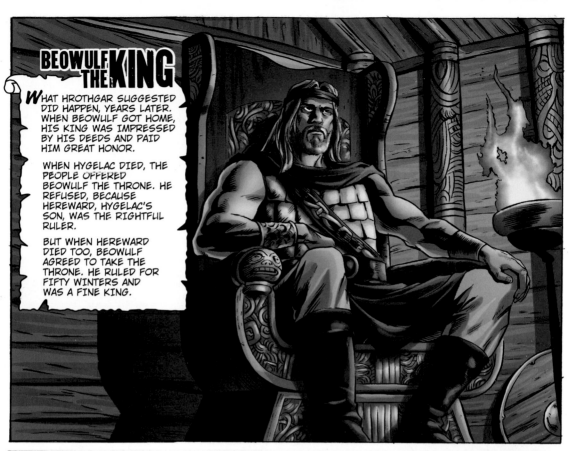

WHAT HROTHGAR SUGGESTED DID HAPPEN, YEARS LATER. WHEN BEOWULF GOT HOME, HIS KING WAS IMPRESSED BY HIS DEEDS AND PAID HIM GREAT HONOR.

WHEN HYGELAC DIED, THE PEOPLE OFFERED BEOWULF THE THRONE. HE REFUSED, BECAUSE HEREWARD, HYGELAC'S SON, WAS THE RIGHTFUL RULER.

BUT WHEN HEREWARD DIED TOO, BEOWULF AGREED TO TAKE THE THRONE. HE RULED FOR FIFTY WINTERS AND WAS A FINE KING.

BUT THEN A DRAGON BEGAN TO RAVAGE THE LAND...

THOUGH NONE KNEW WHY.

BEOWULF WAS SURE HE MUST HAVE ANGERED THE ALMIGHTY. HOW ELSE COULD GOD ALLOW SUCH A DOOM TO FALL UPON HIS PEOPLE?

KNOWING HE MUST FACE THE MONSTER, BEOWULF ORDERED A SHIELD OF IRON FORGED FOR HIM. HE KNEW A WOODEN SHIELD COULD NEVER STAND AGAINST THE DRAGON'S FIERCE FLAME.

BUT BEFORE HE COULD DO BATTLE, HE MUST FIRST FIND THE FIEND.

IT WAS NOT LONG BEFORE ONE OF BEOWULF'S THANES CAME FORWARD TO SOLVE THE MYSTERY OF THE DRAGON'S WRATH.

I WAS DISPLEASED WITH MY SERVANT HERE. HE RAN AWAY TO AVOID MY ANGER.

AS I FLED, I CAME TO AN ANCIENT BARROW. SEEING THE OPEN ARCHWAY, I SLIPPED INSIDE.

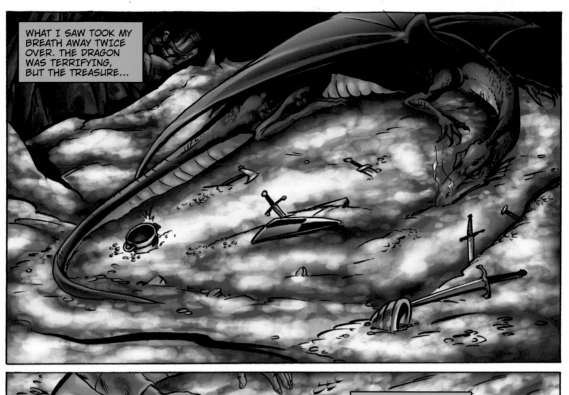

WHAT I SAW TOOK MY BREATH AWAY TWICE OVER. THE DRAGON WAS TERRIFYING, BUT THE TREASURE...

HOPING TO WIN FORGIVENESS WITH A FABULOUS GIFT, I OVERCAME MY FEAR.

I ESCAPED, BUT WHEN THE DRAGON AWOKE...

IT MUST HAVE SEEN THE CUP WAS GONE.

I WAS ALREADY FAR AWAY. IT COULD NOT FIND THE CUP OR ME.

IN ITS RAGE, IT ATTACKED ALL MEN WHO LIVED NEARBY.

35

IF I COULD, I WOULD FACE THIS MONSTER WITH MY BARE HANDS, AS I DID GRENDEL.

BUT I KNOW THAT THERE IS NO SHAME IN NEEDING SWORD, ARMOR, AND SHIELD AGAINST A DRAGON.

ONCE HE LEARNED WHERE THE SERPENT SHELTERED, BEOWULF SET OUT WITH A BAND OF WARRIORS. HE WISHED THE COMPANIONS WHO HAD FACED GRENDEL WITH HIM WERE AT HIS SIDE, BUT NONE WERE LEFT.

I CAN SEE BY THE SMOKE THAT SWIRLS FROM THE DOOR THAT THIS IS THE PLACE OF WHICH THE SERVANT SPOKE.

THIS TASK IS MINE, SO YOU MUST WAIT FOR ME HERE.

THIS CREATURE MAY KILL ME. THEN AGAIN, MAYBE NOT. I HAVE BRAVED MANY BATTLES.

IN MY YOUTH, I GAVE GRENDEL HIS DEATH WOUND. PERHAPS I WILL SLAY THIS SERPENT AND RETURN TO YOU SAFELY.

THE DRAGON

As Beowulf approached the archway, a wave of hot wind beat at his body.

WAKE, WORM, AND MAKE WAR!

ROOOOOOAAAAAAAAAAR!!

BEOWULF KNEW HE COULD NOT FACE THE FIRE FOR LONG.

BEOWULF'S STRENGTH HAD ALWAYS BEEN TOO GREAT FOR IRON TO WITHSTAND.

THOUGH HIS SWORD HAD SNAPPED, THE HERO HELD HIS GROUND.

SEEING BEOWULF IN SUCH DANGER, HIS MEN LOST HEART. ONLY WIGLAF, WEOHSTAN'S SON, DID NOT FLEE.

WAIT!!!

WE SWORE TO BEOWULF TO STAND BY HIM!

RIDE! RIDE! IF BEOWULF CANNOT BEAT THE BEAST, THEN NONE OF US HAS A CHANCE!

THE OTHERS MAY BREAK THEIR BOND, BUT I WILL NOT!

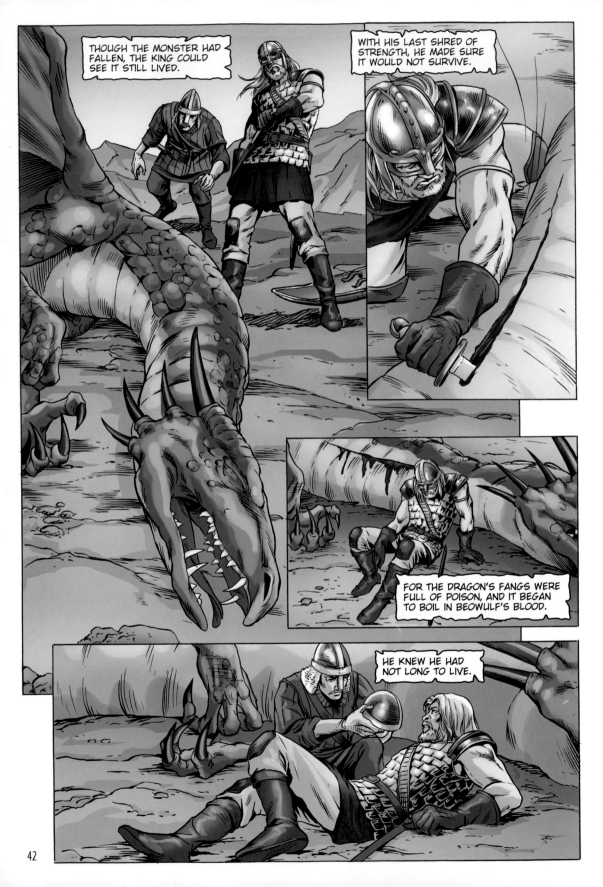

THOUGH THE MONSTER HAD FALLEN, THE KING COULD SEE IT STILL LIVED.

WITH HIS LAST SHRED OF STRENGTH, HE MADE SURE IT WOULD NOT SURVIVE.

FOR THE DRAGON'S FANGS WERE FULL OF POISON, AND IT BEGAN TO BOIL IN BEOWULF'S BLOOD.

HE KNEW HE HAD NOT LONG TO LIVE.

"I ONLY WISH I HAD A SON, SO I COULD SEND MY SWORD AND ARMOR TO HIM."

"BUT MY LIFE WAS LONG, AND I RULED WELL."

"FAITHFUL WIGLAF, WE BOUGHT THE HOARD WITH BRAVERY AND BLOOD."

"IT WILL EASE MY PASSING TO LOOK ON IT. BRING IT OUT WHERE I CAN SEE."

QUICKLY AS HE COULD, WIGLAF DID WHAT HIS KING COMMANDED.

BUT EVEN VICTORY AND TREASURE COULD NOT EASE HIS HEAVY HEART.

GLOSSARY AND PRONUNCIATION GUIDE

BARROW: a mound of dirt or stones that marks a person's burial place

BEOWULF (BAY-uh-wulf): the warrior hero of *Beowulf*, an Old English epic from A.D. 700–800

DRAGON: a scaly, serpentlike creature from mythology. Many countries have stories about dragons. In China and Japan, they are symbols of good luck. But in European mythology, dragons are dangerous, fire-breathing killers. In English myths, they are sometimes called worms.

ECGTHEOW (EDGE-theh-ow): Beowulf's father

ENCHANTMENT: a magical spell that influences the physical world, either by causing something to happen or by preventing it

FENS: wetlands usually covered by pools of water, grasses, and reeds

GEATLAND (yay-AHT-lond): a region in the southwestern corner of modern Sweden

GEATS (yay-AHTS): people from Geatland. Beowulf and his soldiers were Geats.

HELM: a metal helmet worn in battle

HEOROT (HAIR-ut): King Hrothgar's mead hall

HERALD: a person who carries messages and announces information

HILT: the end of a sword used as a handgrip

HROTHGAR (HRAHTH-gahr): a king of Denmark

HRUNTING (HRUN-ting): the sword given to Beowulf by Unferth

HYGELAC (HOO-yuh-lahk): the king of the Geats

MAIL: a material used in making medieval soldiers' protective gear, such as byrnies. Mail was made from small circles of hammered metal linked together to form a fabric. Mail is often called chain mail.

MEAD: an alcoholic drink made from honey and fruit

MEAD HALL: a gathering place for dining and socializing

THANE: a king's attendant. Thanes were usually soldiers to whom the king gave land in return for military service.

FURTHER READING AND WEBSITES

The Anglo-Saxons
http://www.bbc.co.uk/schools/anglosaxons/index.shtml
    The "Schools" section of the British Broadcasting Corporation's homepage
    features a history of the Anglo-Saxons. How the Anglo-Saxons came to the
    British Isles, how they lived, what religious beliefs they held, and other facets
    of Anglo-Saxon life are discussed. Each topic includes links to a glossary.

Beowulf
http://www.bl.uk/onlinegallery/themes/englishlit/beowulf.html
    The Online Gallery of the British Library features information about the last
    remaining copy of the original *Beowulf* manuscript and a brief explanation of
    the epic poem's importance to English literature. The gallery also features an
    image of a page from the one-thousand-year-old manuscript.

Crossley-Holland, Kevin. *Beowulf*. Illustrated by Charles Keeping. Oxford:
    Oxford University Press, 1987. Crossley-Holland retells the Anglo-Saxon
    epic in prose for young readers. The story is accompanied by Keeping's black-
    and-white illustrations.

CREATING *BEOWULF: MONSTER SLAYER*

In creating the story, author Paul D. Storrie used well-known translations of
Beowulf, including the translation (with introduction) by Burton Raffel, the
Donaldson translation (with background, sources, and criticism) edited by Joseph
F. Tuso, and an Oxford University Press translation by Ian Serraillier. Artist
Ron Randall used sources on Anglo-Saxon armaments, ships, clothing, and
architecture to shape the story's visual details. Consultant Andrew Scheil of the
University of Minnesota provided expert guidance on historical details, textual
accuracy, and Anglo-Saxon pronunciation.

original pencil from page 39

INDEX

Westfield Memorial Library
Westfield, New Jersey

ABOUT THE AUTHOR AND THE ARTIST

PAUL D. STORRIE was born and raised in Detroit, Michigan. He has returned to live there again and again after living in other cities and states. He began writing professionally in 1987 and has written comics for Caliber Comics, Moonstone Books, Marvel Comics, and DC Comics. His Graphic Myths and Legends work includes *Hercules: The Twelve Labors*; *Robin Hood: Outlaw of Sherwood Forest*; *Yu the Great: Conquering the Flood*; and *Amaterasu: Return of the Sun*. He had also written *Robyn of Sherwood* (featuring stories about Robin Hood's daughter); *Batman Beyond*; *Gotham Girls*; *Captain America: Red, White and Blue*; *Mutant X*; and *Revisionary*.

RON RANDALL has drawn comics for every major comic publisher in the United States, including Marvel, DC, Image, and Dark Horse. His Graphic Myths and Legends work includes *Thor & Loki: In the Land of Giants* and *Amaterasu: Return of the Sun*. He has also worked on superhero comics such as *Justice League* and *Spiderman*; science fiction titles such as *Star Wars* and *Star Trek*; fantasy adventure titles such as *DragonLance* and *Warlord*; suspense and horror titles including *SwampThing*, *Predator*, and *Venom*; and his own creation, *Trekker*. He lives in Portland, Oregon.